TRICKY JOURNEYS #6

TRICKY MONKEY TALES

CHRIS SCHWEIZER

ILLUSTRATED BY CHAD THOMAS

GRAPHIC UNIVERSE™ • MINNEAPOLIS • NEW YORK

Story by Chris Schweizer

Illustrations by Chad Thomas

Coloring by John Novak

Lettering by Grace Lu

Copyright © 2011 by Lerner Publishing Group, Inc.

Graphic Universe™ and Tricky Journeys™ are trademarks of Lerner Publishing Group, Inc.

Graphic Universe™
A division of Lerner Publishing Group, Inc.
241 First Avenue North
Minneapolis, MN 55401 U.S.A.

Website address: www.lernerbooks.com

Main body text set in CC Dave Gibbons Lower 14/22.
Typeface provided by Comicraft/Active Images.

Library of Congress Cataloging-in-Publication Data

Schweizer, Chris.
   Tricky Monkey tales / by Chris Schweizer ; illustrated by Chad Thomas.
     p. cm. — (Tricky journeys)
   Summary: Monkey, a trickster, encounters many other creatures, some friendly and some dangerous, and the reader makes choices that help keep Monkey out of harm's way.
   ISBN: 978-0-7613-6611-9 (lib. bdg. : alk. paper)
   1. Plot-your-own stories. 2. Graphic novels. [1. Graphic novels. 2. Monkeys—Fiction. 3. Tricksters—Fiction. 4. Animals—Fiction. 5. Plot-your-own stories.] I. Thomas, Chad, ill. II. Title.
PZ7.7.S39Tqm 2011
741.5'973—dc22   2011000366

Manufactured in the United States of America
1 – CG – 7/15/11

Are you ready for your Tricky Journeys™? You'll find yourself right smack in the middle of this story's tricks, jokes, thrills, and fun. Each page tells what happens to Monkey and his friends. **YOU** get to decide what happens next. Read each page until you reach a choice. Then pick the choice **YOU** like best. But be careful...one wrong choice could land Monkey in a mess even he can't trick his way out of!

Monkey yawns as he sits on his throne. A servant brings him grapes, but he shoos them away. "What is the matter, Prince Monkey?" asks the servant.

"I'm bored!" says Monkey. "Everyone always brings me whatever I want."

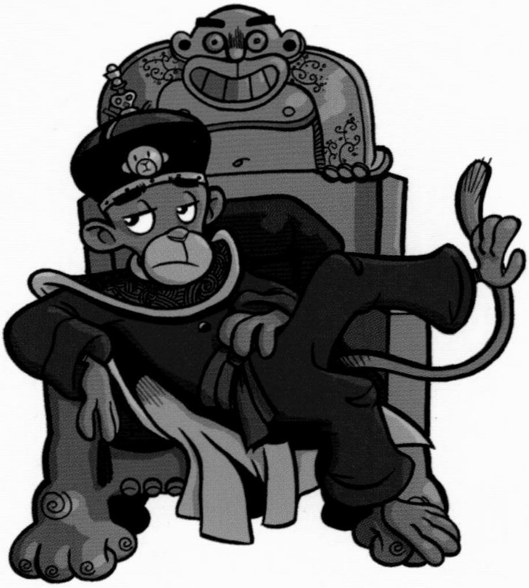

"Of course we do," says the servant. "You're the prince! As long as you stay in the palace, your every need will be cared for."

"As long as I stay . . ." repeats Monkey. He watches the servant leave, then jumps to his feet.

 Go on to the next page.

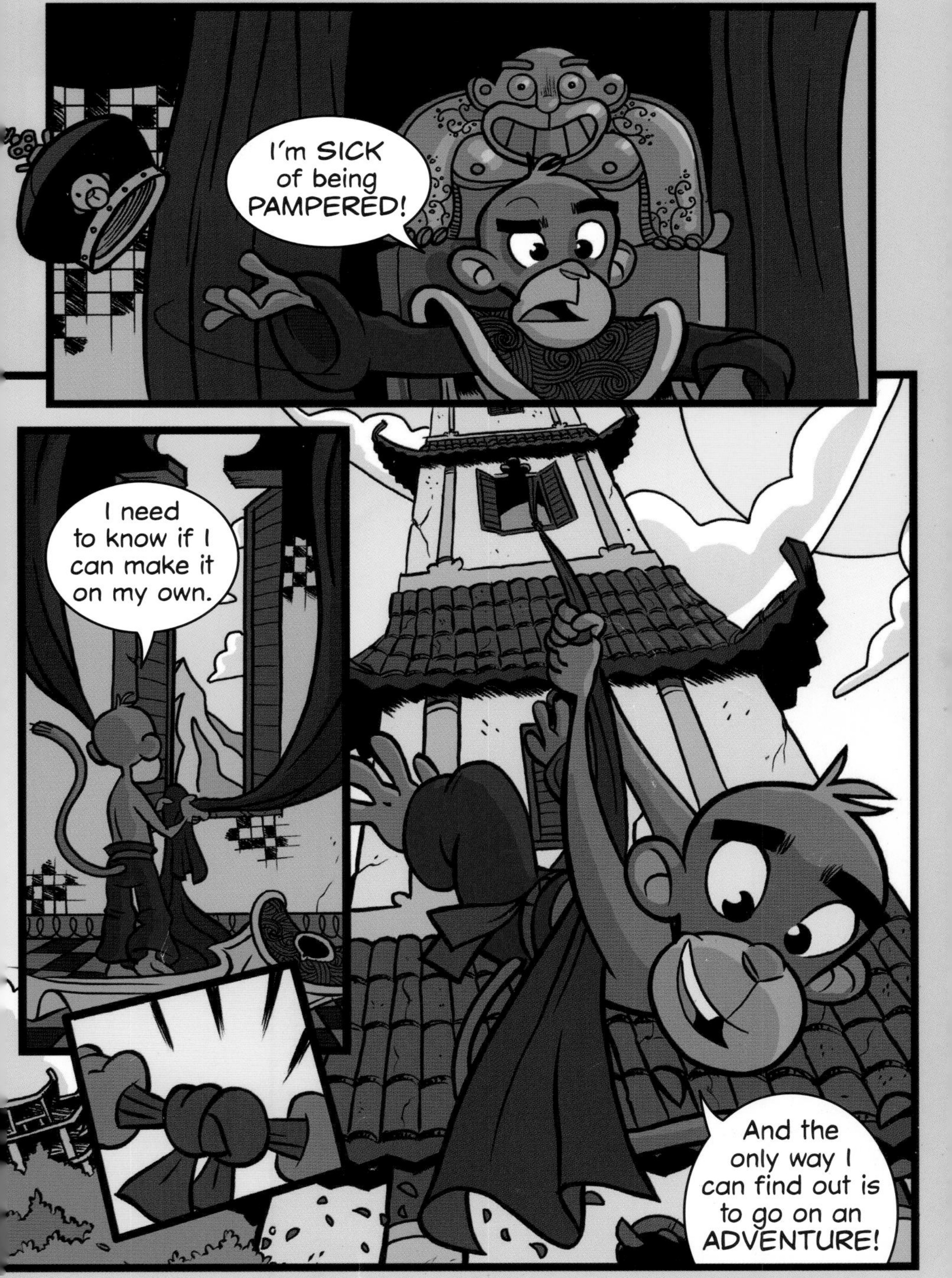
I'm SICK of being PAMPERED!
I need to know if I can make it on my own.
And the only way I can find out is to go on an ADVENTURE!

Go on to the next page.

Monkey lands outside. "Now I just need to find the most exciting place to have an adventure," he says to himself.

If Monkey goes to the mountains,

TURN TO PAGE **30.**

If Monkey goes to the sea,

TURN TO PAGE **46.**

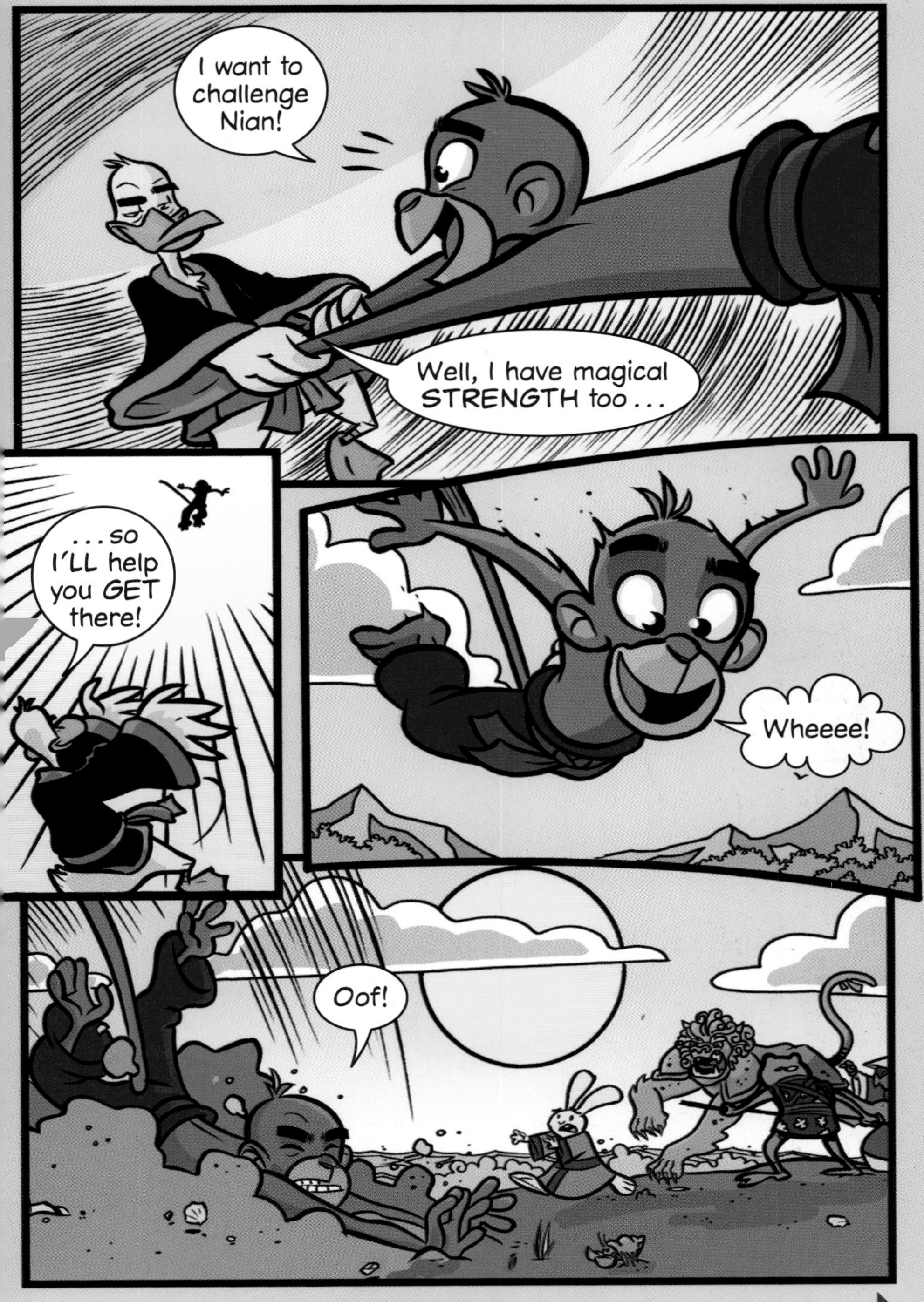
I want to challenge Nian!
Well, I have magical STRENGTH too . . .
. . . so I'LL help you GET there!
Wheeee!
Oof!

Go on to the next page.

"Nian is attacking that village!" says Monkey. "I have to stop him!"

If Monkey grabs Nian by the tail,

TURN TO PAGE 24.

If Monkey jumps into Nian's mouth,

TURN TO PAGE 55.

"Hold your feet apart," says Duck. "Keep them planted. Tilt to your right, and the cloud goes to the right. Tilt to the left, and it goes to your left. Do you understand?"

Monkey nods.

"All right," says Duck. "You are ready to go. Enjoy yourself."

Monkey waves and zips away. He flies around trees. He shoots over a hill. On the other side he sees a giant! Monkey swerves to avoid him.

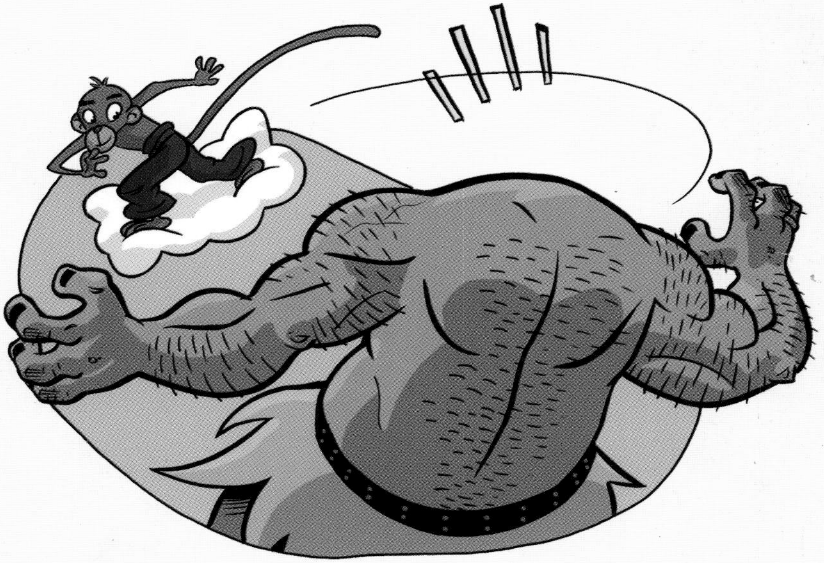

Go on to the next page.

"Who dares to trespass on the cliff of mighty Xing?" bellows the giant. Monkey gasps. He's heard of Xing. Xing is a cruel and terrible monster.

If Monkey tries to fight Xing,

TURN TO PAGE 27.

If Monkey tries to get away,

TURN TO PAGE 62.

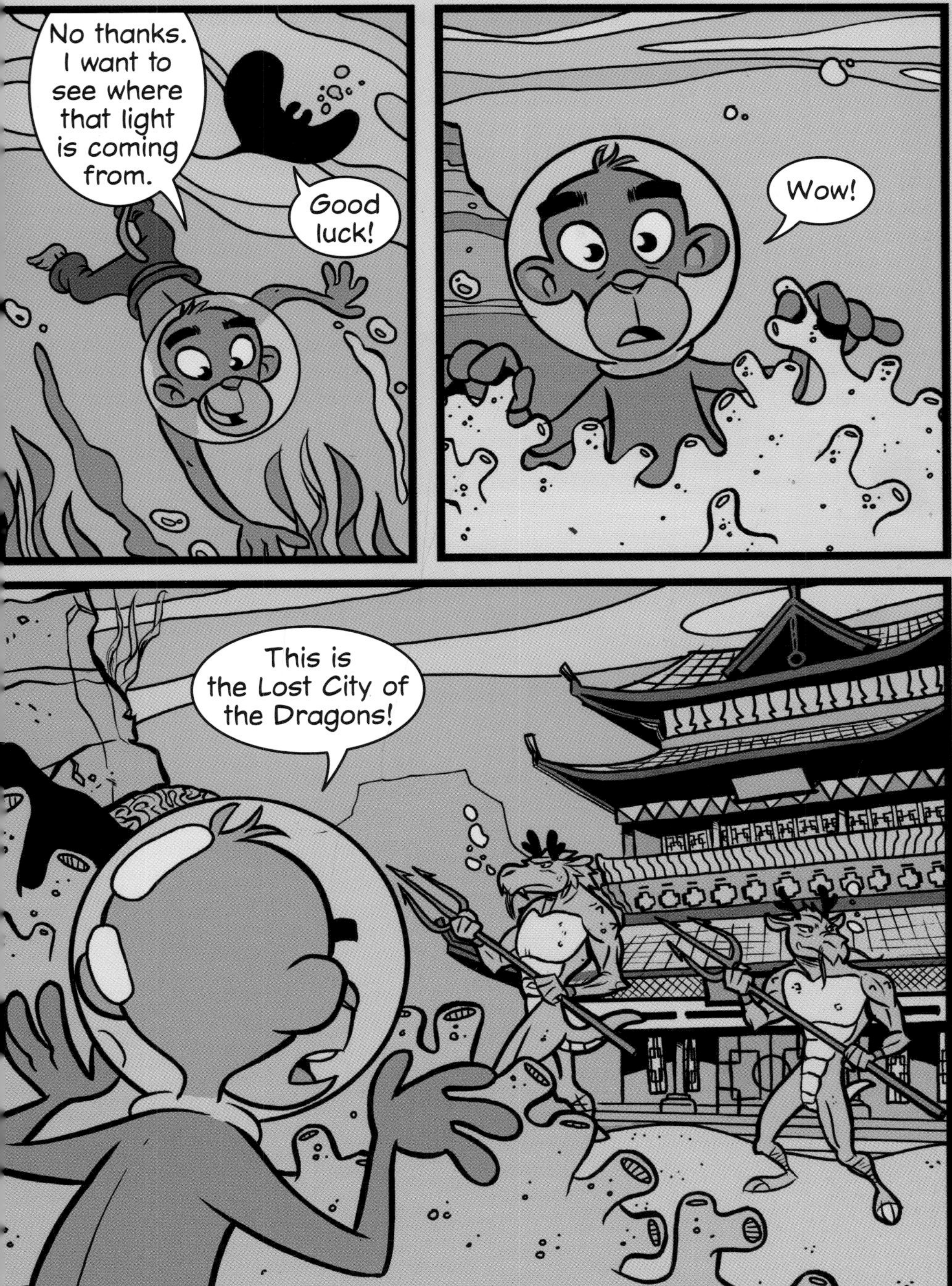
No thanks. I want to see where that light is coming from.
Good luck!
Wow!
This is the Lost City of the Dragons!

"Yikes! Those guards look pretty dangerous!" thinks Monkey. "But no one has seen real dragons in hundreds of years! Maybe I should take a closer look."

If Monkey swims down to check out the city,

TURN TO PAGE 51.

If Monkey swims away to avoid the dragon guards,

TURN TO PAGE 33.

"Excuse me," says Monkey. "I made that sundae for myself. You have changing powers. If you want one, you should make your own."

The duck looks angry. "That's a wonderful idea!" he quacks. With a "pop!" Duck transforms Monkey into an enormous banana split!

"Young people these days are so ungrateful," mumbles Duck. He takes a big spoonful of chocolate-covered banana.

THE END

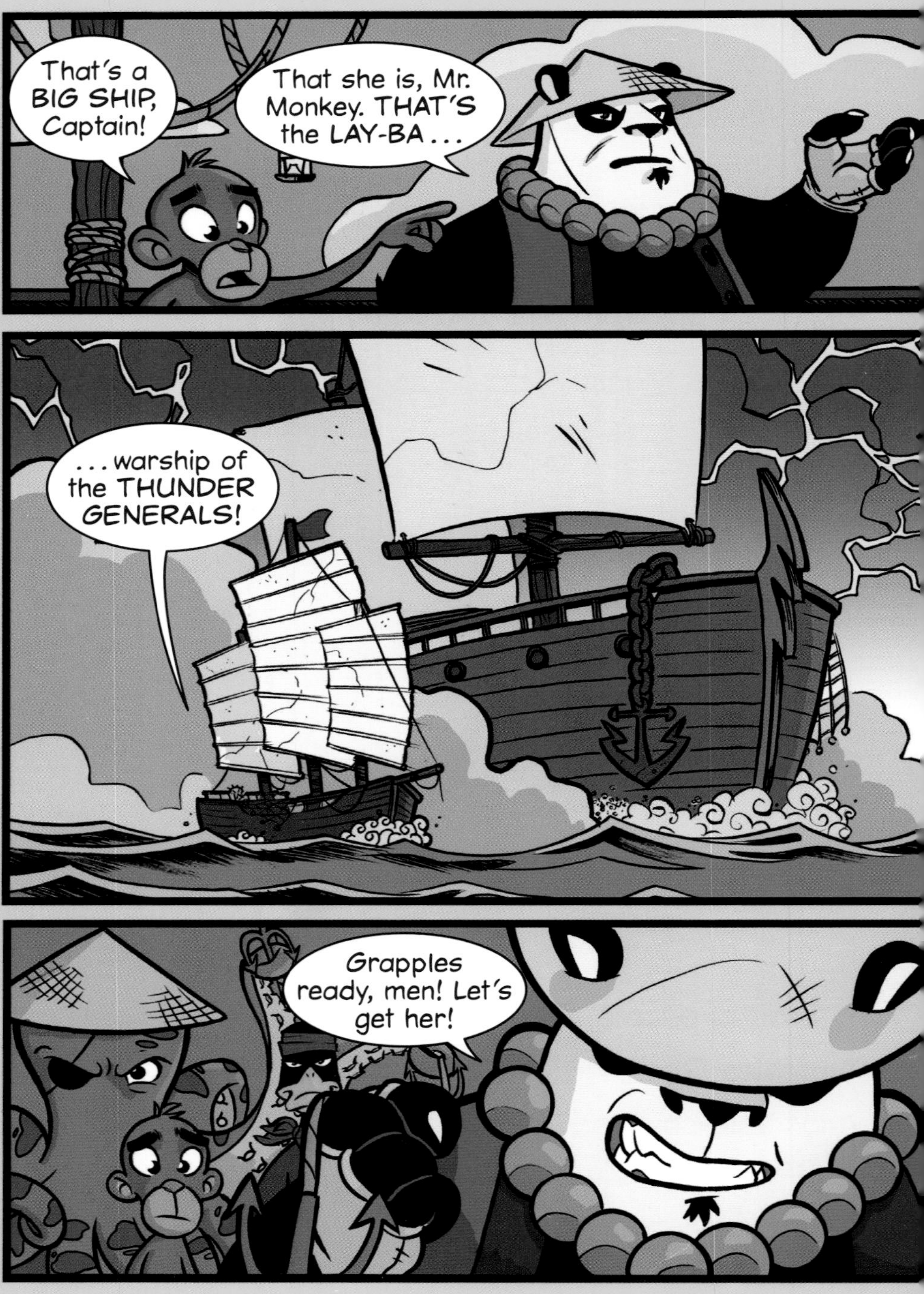
That's a BIG SHIP, Captain!
That she is, Mr. Monkey. THAT'S the LAY-BA . . .
. . . warship of the THUNDER GENERALS!
Grapples ready, men! Let's get her!

The pirates swing onto the warship. The soldiers on deck scatter at the sight of the pirates. Then a giant door to the inside of the ship swings open. Three huge creatures walk out.

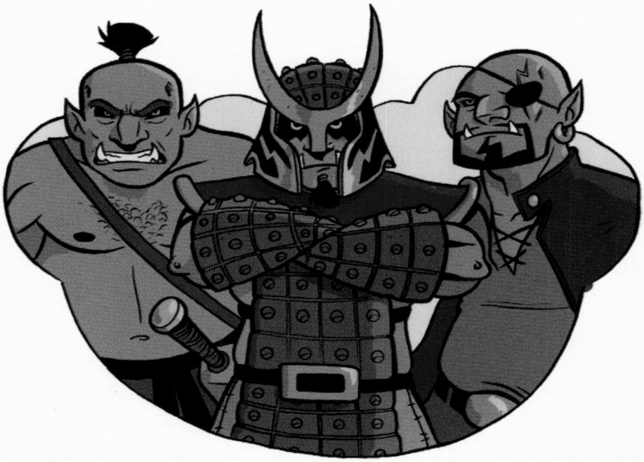

"It's the Thunder Generals!" yells Captain Panda. "Prepare for battle!"

One of the generals swings his club. A loud crack of thunder travels across the deck. Goose and Lizard go flying overboard. The one-eyed general aims his club at Monkey!

"Your turn," he bellows.

Go on to the next page.

Monkey jumps in the air as the general's thunderclap rips through the mast behind him. The general will smash him to dust if he doesn't act fast!

If Monkey tries to cover the general's good eye,

TURN TO PAGE 61.

If Monkey tricks the general into attacking him,

TURN TO PAGE 34.

Monkey picks up another rock and changes it into a spoon. Then he starts to eat! He eats for hours, enjoying the creamy banana flavor.

Monkey is still eating when he hears a CREAK. He looks up and sees the tower of ice cream swaying. He's eaten through almost the entire bottom!

Monkey jumps to his feet. He starts running just as the tower starts to topple over. He'd better run fast!

THE END

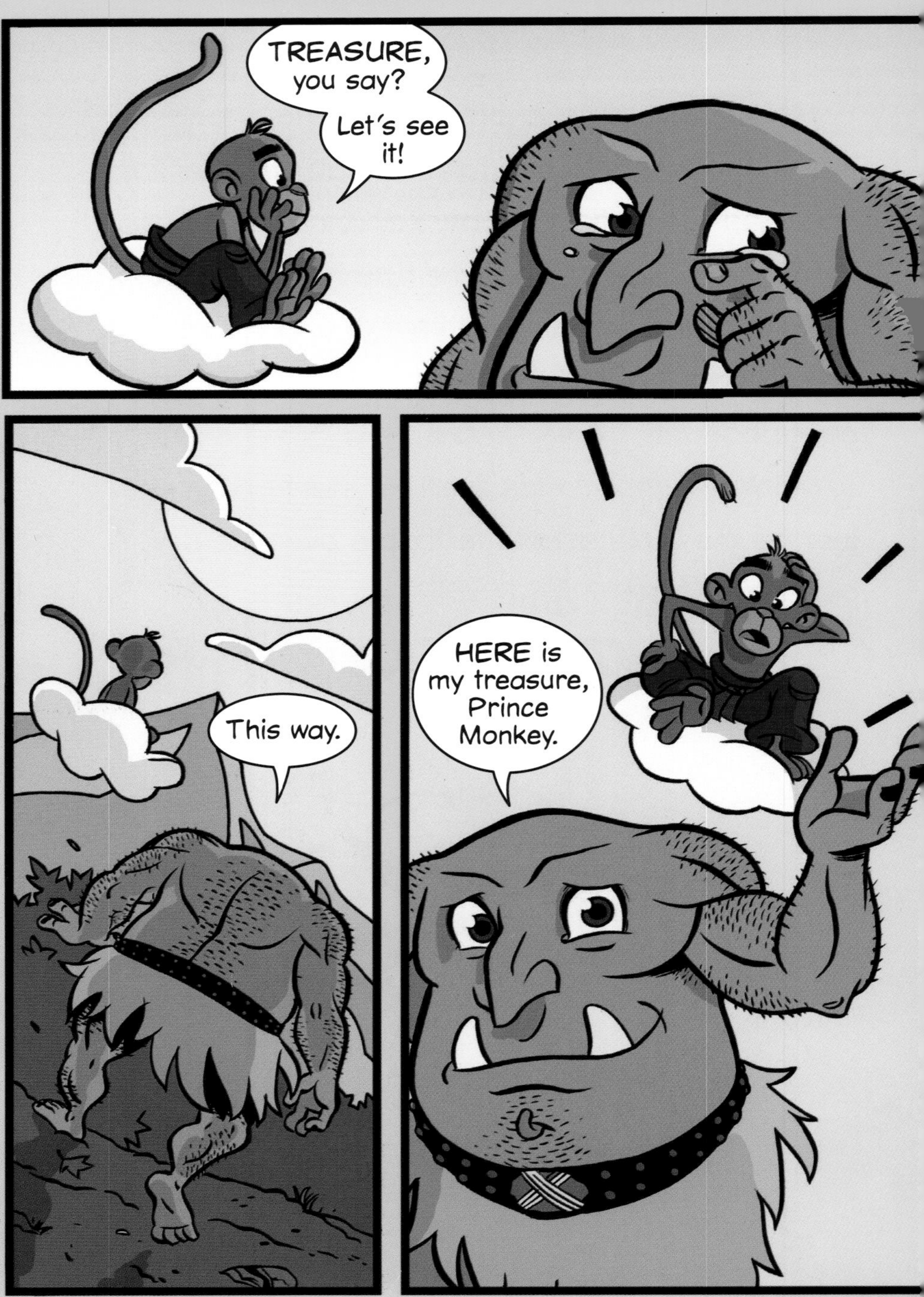
TREASURE, you say?
Let's see it!
This way.
HERE is my treasure, Prince Monkey.

Go on to the next page.

On the ground are a dozen small animals. "These are my friends," says Xing. "Friends are the greatest treasure a person can have."

Monkey looks confused. "But you're supposed to be a cruel monster!" he says.

Xing laughs. "I just act scary to keep bigger animals away. These guys are so small. I want to keep them safe. But if you'll be nice, then you can be friends with us too."

Monkey smiles. That sounds good to him!

THE END

"I won't let you attack innocent animals," says Monkey. He grabs the ship's wheel and steers it away from the other boat.

"How dare you!" yells Captain Panda, drawing his sword. Panda swings it at Monkey. Monkey ducks. Panda swings it again. The second time, it comes a lot closer to hitting Monkey.

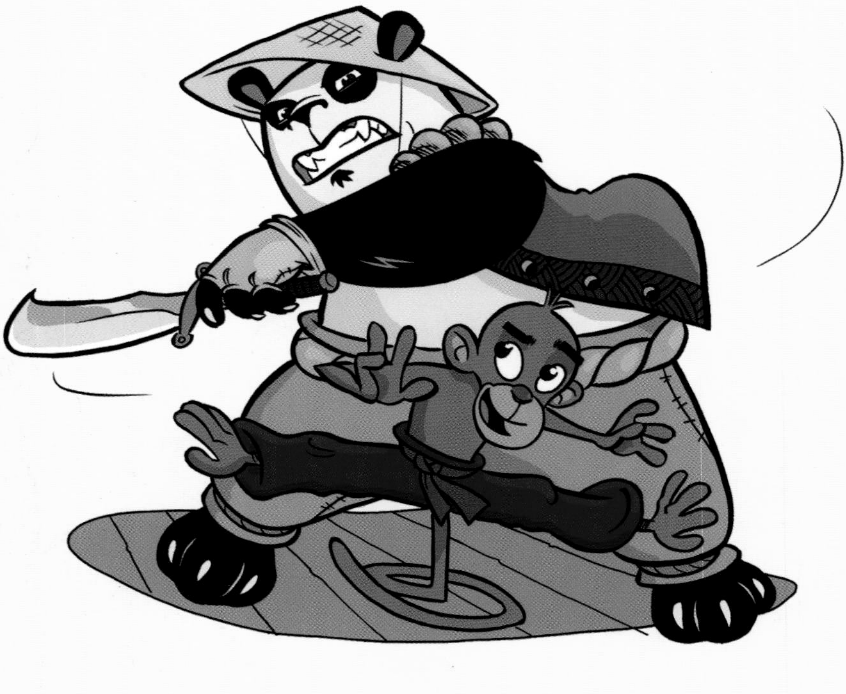

 Go on to the next page.

Monkey had better act fast if he doesn't want to end up sliced in two!

If Monkey tries to take command of the pirate ship,

TURN TO PAGE **40.**

If Monkey tries to swim to the other ship,

TURN TO PAGE **25.**

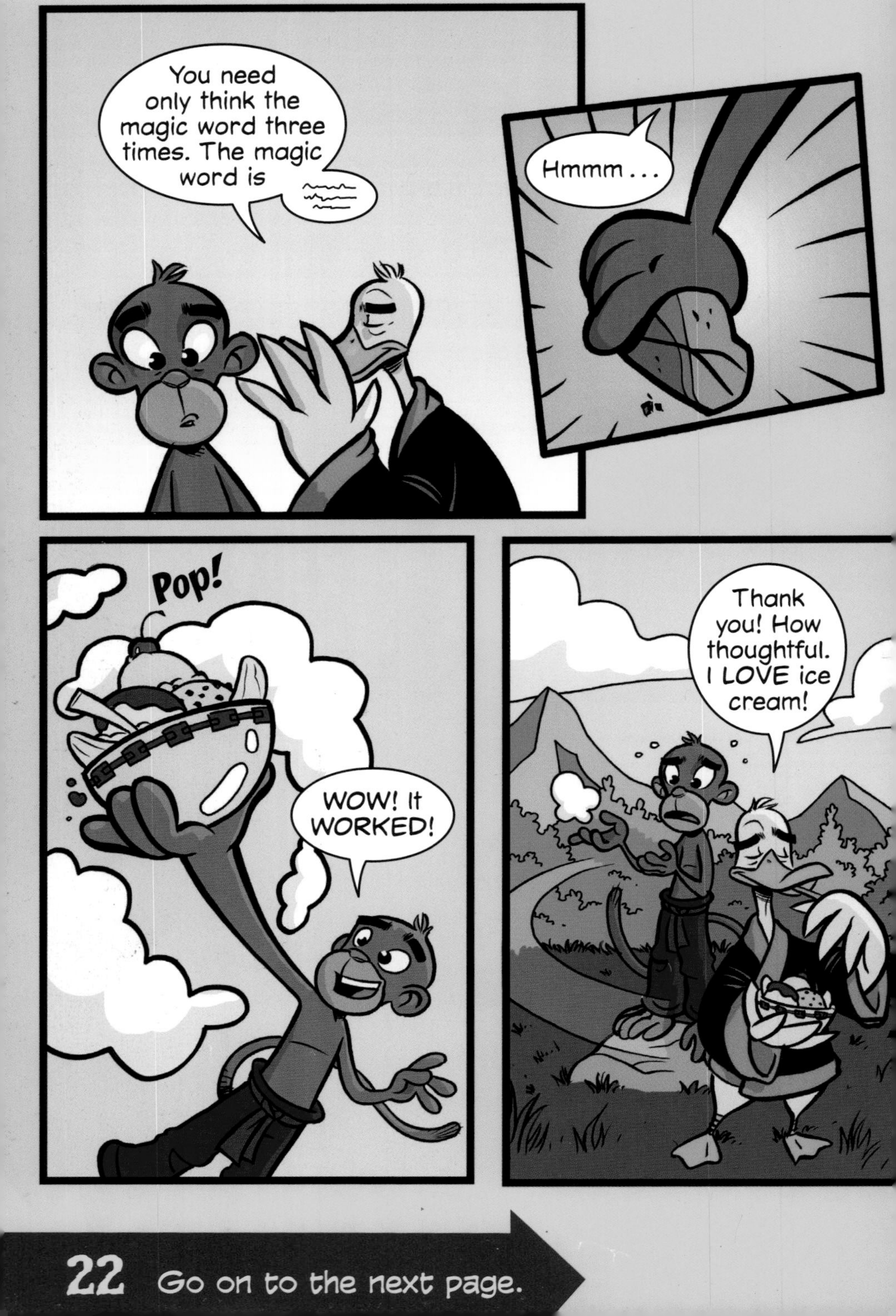
You need only think the magic word three times. The magic word is
Hmmm . . .
Pop!
WOW! It WORKED!
Thank you! How thoughtful. I LOVE ice cream!

 Go on to the next page.

Monkey can't believe that this old duck would steal his ice cream! Then again, the duck did teach him a valuable skill.

If Monkey asks for his ice cream back,

TURN TO PAGE 13.

If Monkey says "you're welcome" to Duck,

TURN TO PAGE 59.

Monkey grabs Nian's tail. Nian looks back and roars. He slams his tail down on the ground. Then he lifts it and slams it again. Monkey holds on tight. Nian's mighty blows don't hurt him at all.

Nian keeps smacking his tail, trying to shake free from Monkey. Soon he is so tired that he passes out right on the beach.

Monkey has stopped Nian. But invulnerable or not, he could use a rest himself!

THE END

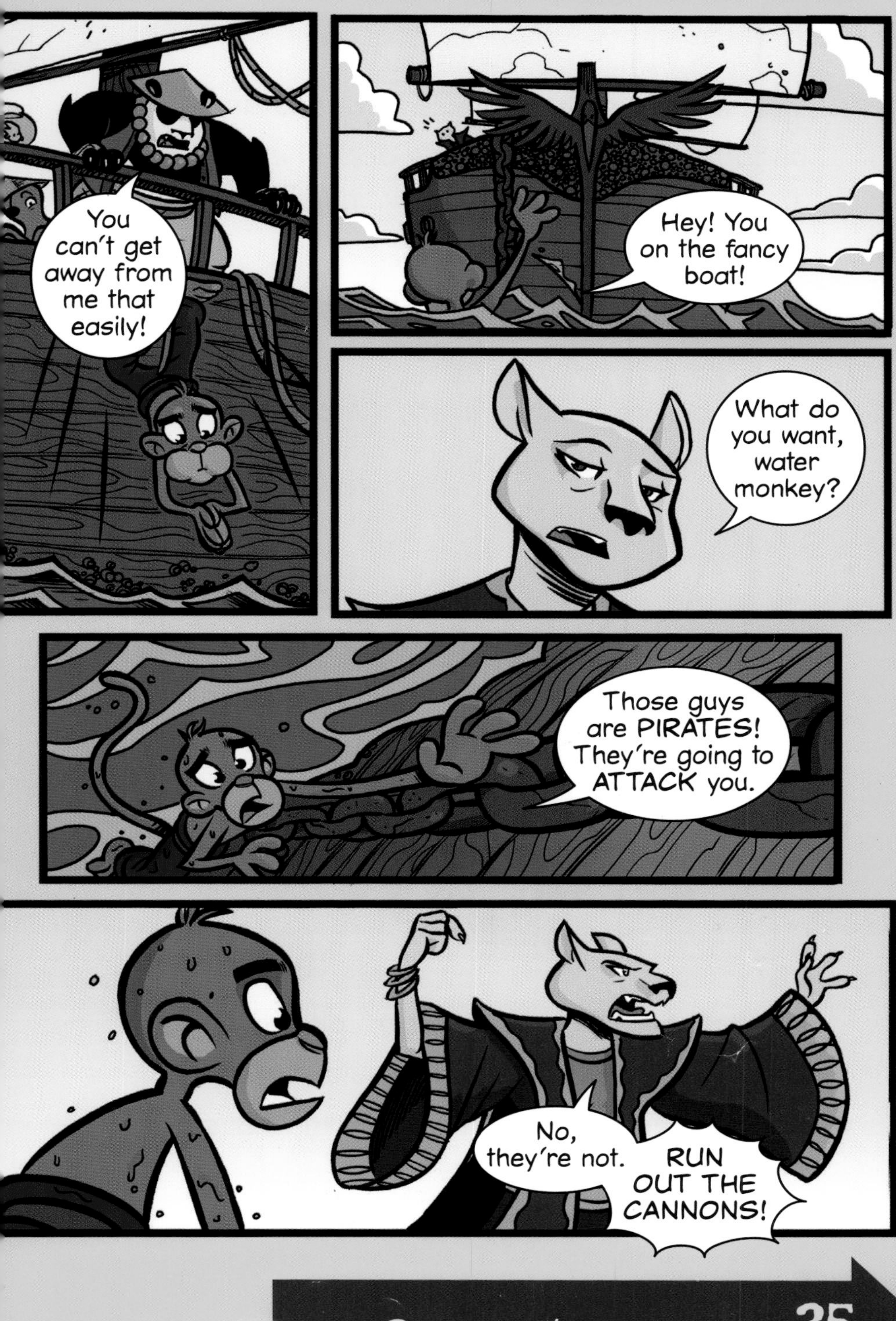
You can't get away from me that easily!
Hey! You on the fancy boat!
What do you want, water monkey?
Those guys are PIRATES! They're going to ATTACK you.
No, they're not.
RUN OUT THE CANNONS!

The side of the fancy ship opens and
hundreds of cannons slide out. The pirates
see that they're outmatched. They sail away
as fast as they can.

"Wow!" says Monkey. "It looks like you guys
can take care of yoursel—"

But before he can finish, the panther slams a
big vase over his head!

"You might be a pirate too," she says. "I'm
taking you to jail." Monkey would explain, but his
words simply echo in the vase. His adventure
has reached

THE END

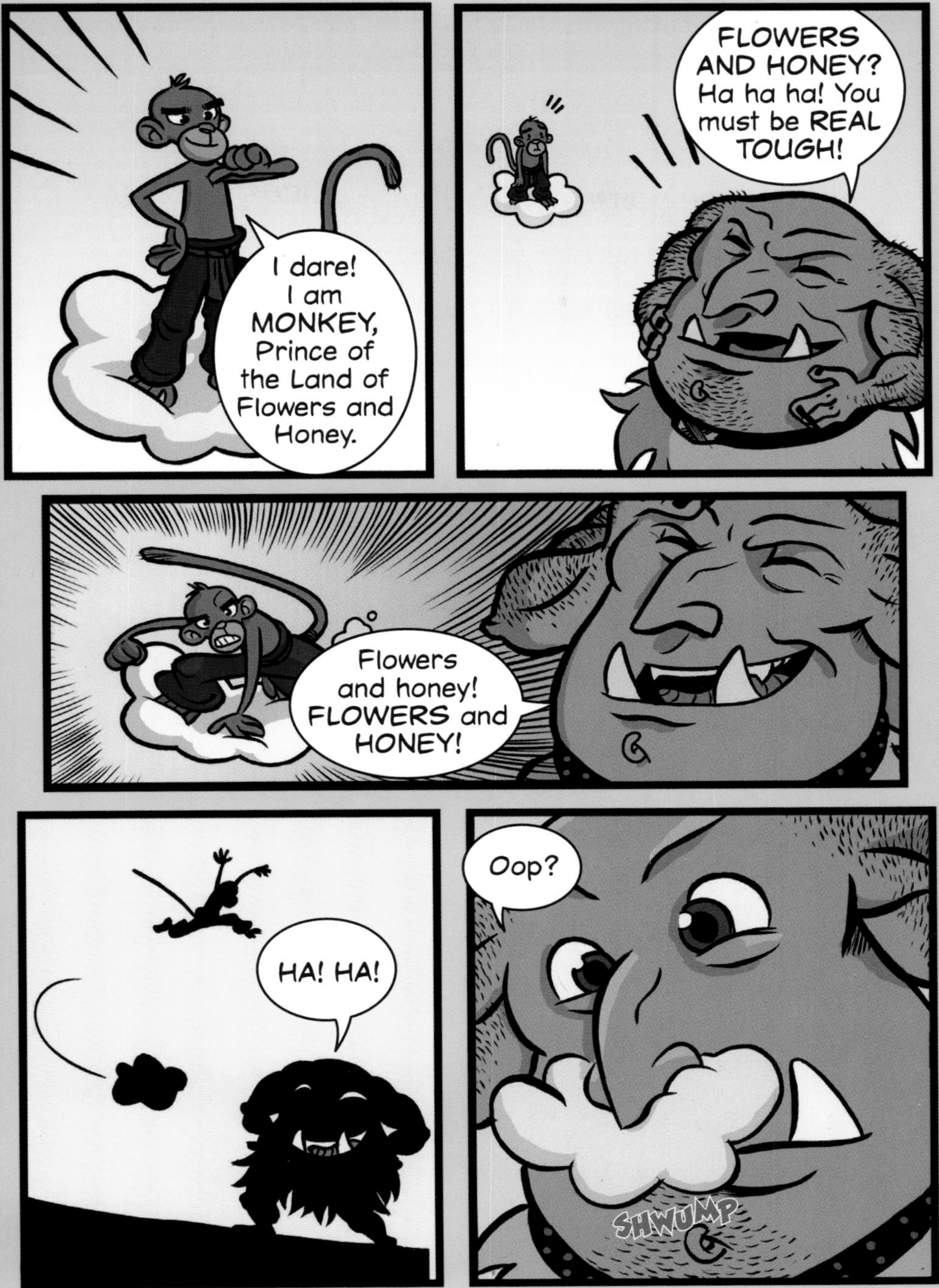
I dare! I am MONKEY, Prince of the Land of Flowers and Honey.
FLOWERS AND HONEY? Ha ha ha! You must be REAL TOUGH!
Flowers and honey! FLOWERS and HONEY!
HA! HA!
Oop?
SHWUMP

Go on to the next page.

Monkey lands lightly on Xing's head. Xing staggers backward, batting at his face. "By dode! Your cloud stobbed ub by dode!"

"I can't understand you," says Monkey, laughing.

If Monkey calls another cloud down to help him defeat Xing,

TURN TO PAGE 42.

If Monkey makes Xing fall off the cliff,

TURN TO PAGE 56.

Monkey takes a leap off the side of the mountain. He falls down, down, down. Finally, he lands. He isn't hurt!

"Wow!" he says, dusting himself off. "I can't wait to use my new skill out on the road."

Monkey looks around. He has fallen into a deep pit! He tries to climb, but the walls are too steep. Monkey survived the fall. But now he's trapped...

Forever!

THE END

Monkey walks for a long time. Finally, he gets to the base of the mountain and starts to climb. He is partway up when he hears a cry for help. It's a little old duck, quacking in terror. A snow leopard is stalking toward the bird!

"Hey," cries Monkey. "Leave that duck alone!"

The leopard turns. "Certainly!" he says. "I'd much rather snack on a young monkey!" He pounces at Monkey!

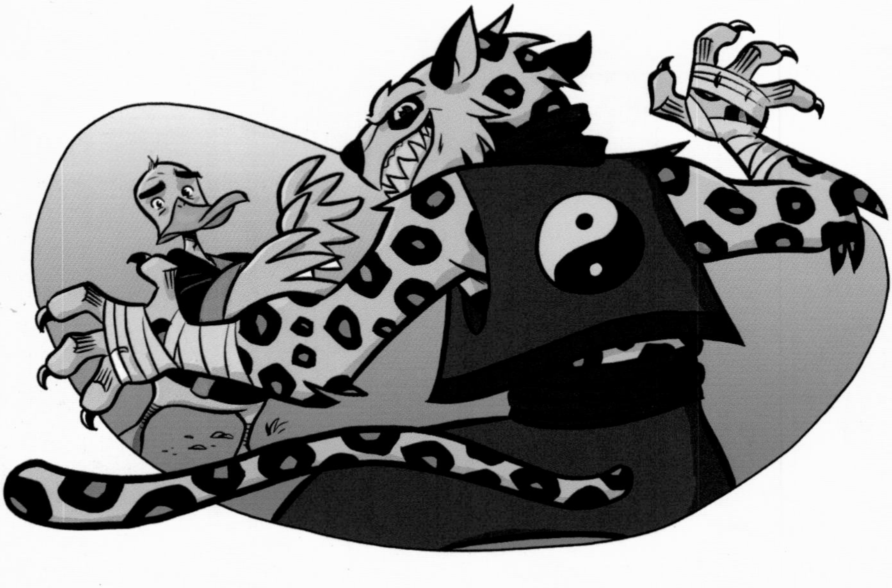

Go on to the next page.

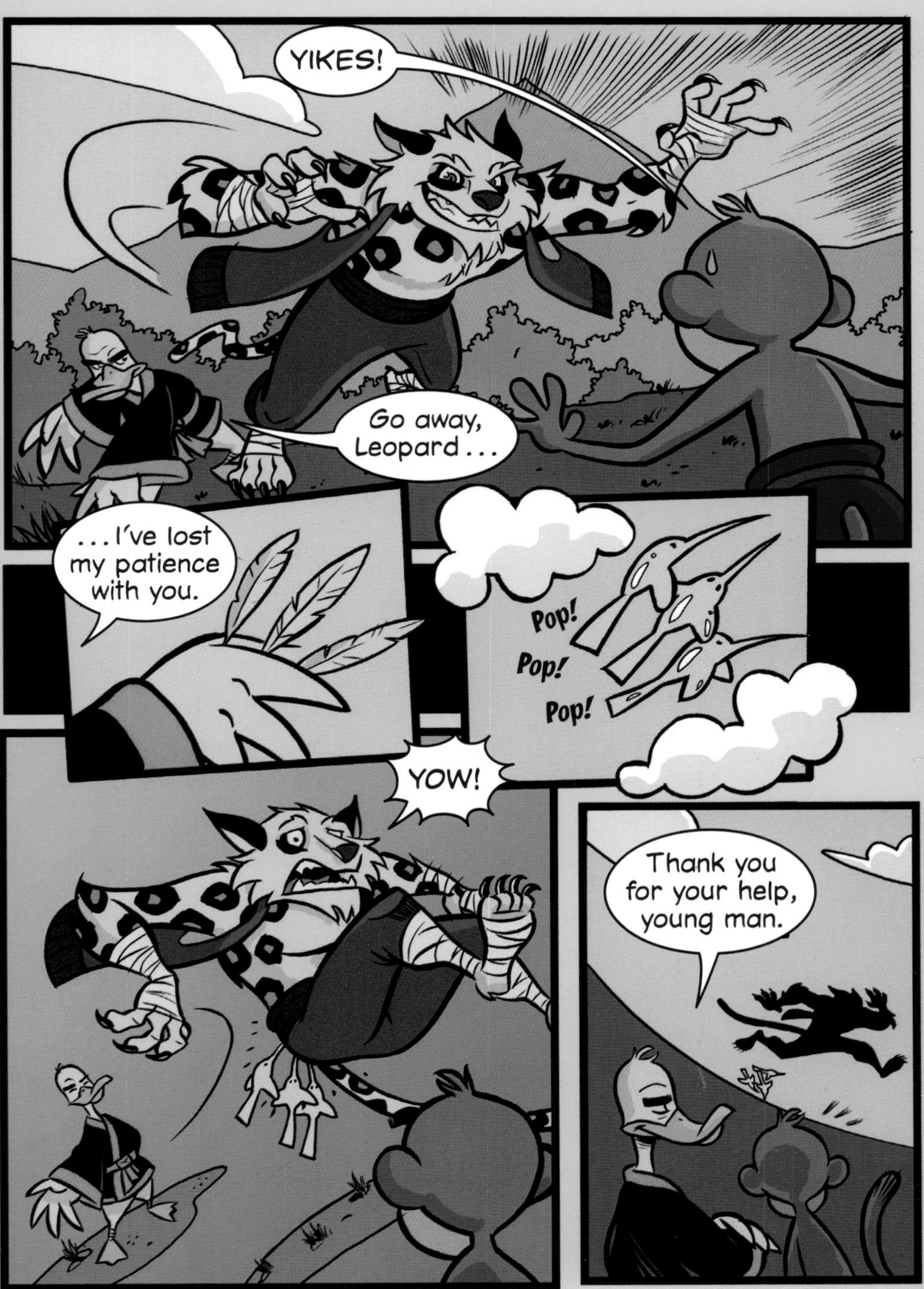
YIKES!
Go away, Leopard . . .
. . . I've lost my patience with you.
Pop!
Pop!
Pop!
YOW!
Thank you for your help, young man.

"To thank you," Duck says, "I will teach you one of my magical powers: cloud riding, changing one thing into another, or invulnerability."

"What does INVULNERABILITY mean?" asks Monkey.

"It means that you can't be hurt," replies Duck.

If Monkey wants to learn to ride clouds,

TURN TO PAGE 53.

If Monkey wants to learn to become invulnerable,

TURN TO PAGE 49.

If Monkey wants to learn how to change one thing into another,

TURN TO PAGE 22.

"I'd better get out of here before they see me," thinks Monkey. He turns around to leave and freezes.

Behind him are five dragon guards, all pointing harpoons at him!

"No one looks upon the Lost City of the Dragons and sees the surface world again!" hisses one of the guards.

Soon, Monkey finds himself shackled in a dungeon. He's trapped forever... unless the surface world sends a rescue party!

THE END

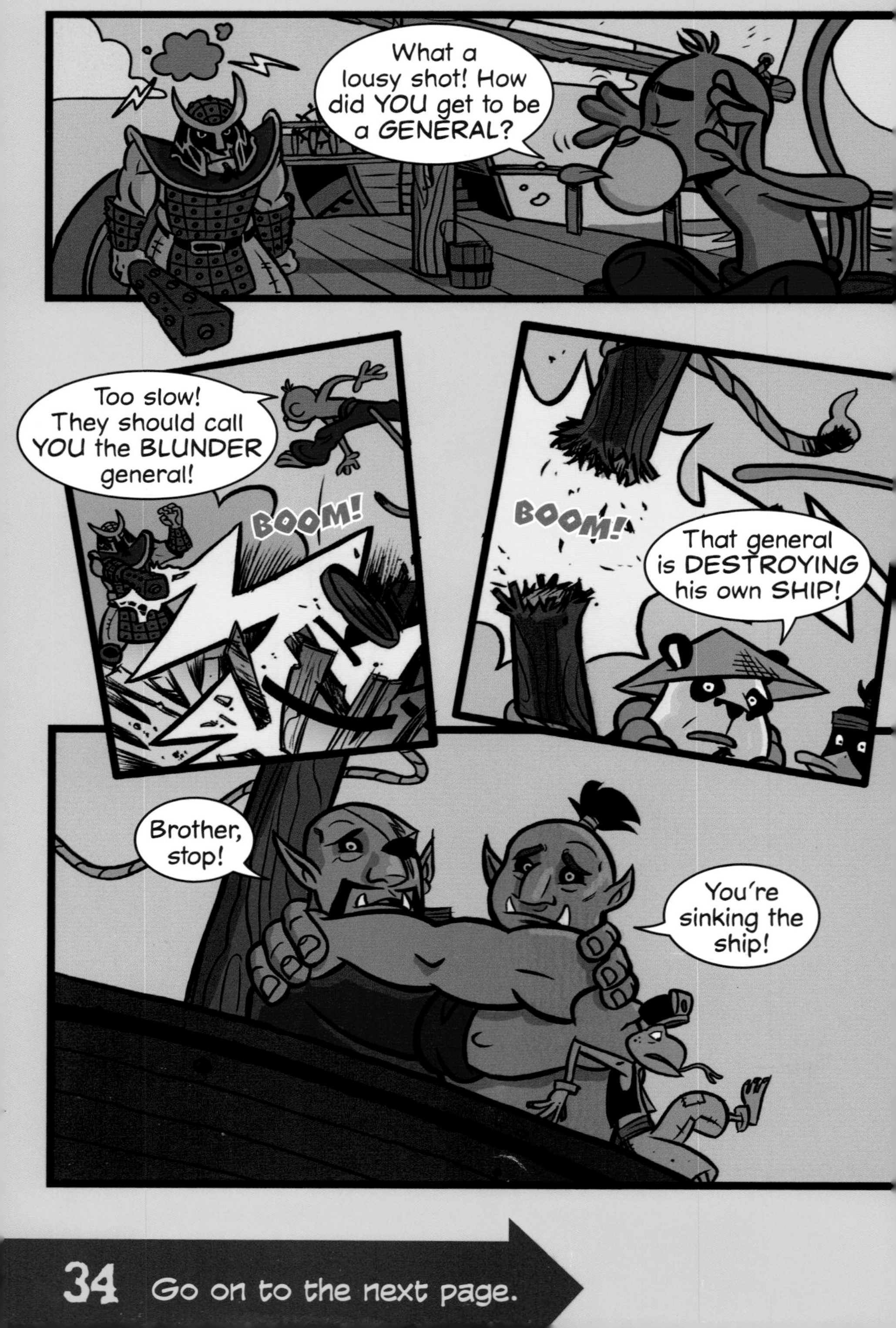
What a lousy shot! How did YOU get to be a GENERAL?
Too slow! They should call YOU the BLUNDER general!
BOOM!
BOOM!
That general is DESTROYING his own SHIP!
Brother, stop!
You're sinking the ship!

Monkey joins the pirates as they swing back to their own ship. "Good work, Mr. Monkey!" says Captain Panda. "The Thunder Generals were coming to conquer our country. Thanks to you, we're free!"

"I'm glad I could help!" says Monkey. "Now I'll be free to live as a pirate. And that's just what I'm going to do!"

THE END

Monkey knows that he's a natural at cloud flying. "I can handle it," he says to Duck. He shoots up into the sky. He squints as the wind rushes past his face. He's going faster than he ever imagined.

Then his feet start to slide down into the cloud. Soon the cloud is up to Monkey's chest. It's fading away into mist!

"I told you not to go so fast," says Duck. But Monkey can't hear him. He's too busy falling.

THE END

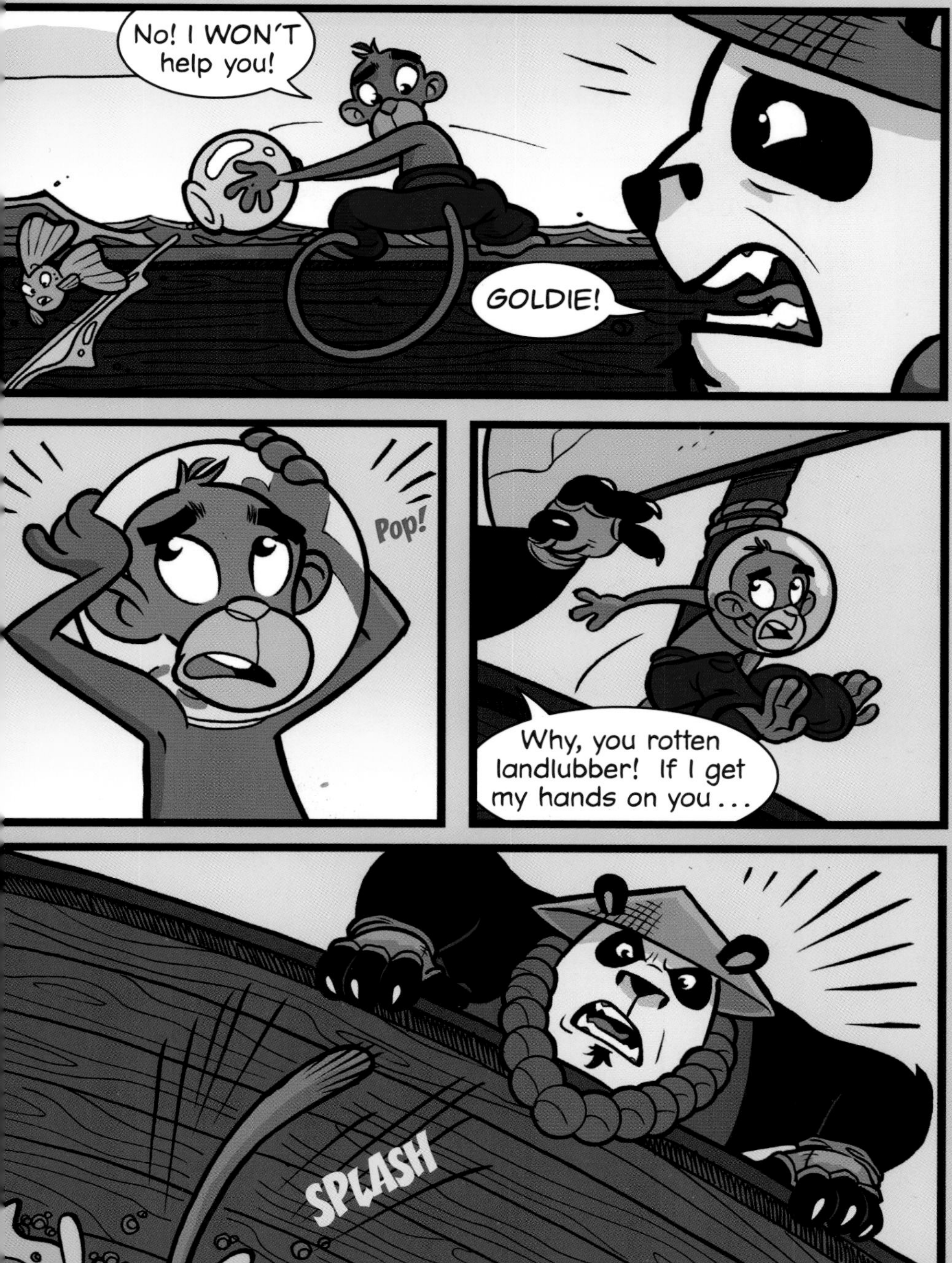
No! I WON'T help you!
GOLDIE!
Pop!
Why, you rotten landlubber! If I get my hands on you . . .
SPLASH

Monkey sees a bright light below. What could it be? He's about to investigate when a manta ray swoops around in front of him. "Hello, little not-fish," says Manta Ray. "Can I give you a lift?"

If Monkey accepts Manta Ray's offer,

TURN TO PAGE 58.

If Monkey investigates the light,

TURN TO PAGE 11.

"No deal," says Monkey. He gives Xing a final smack. Xing falls off the cliff! Monkey laughs with pride.

"Shame on you," says a voice. Monkey turns his head. It's Duck.

"You're a bully," says the old bird. "I never should have taught you to ride. Luckily, I didn't teach you how to stay on a RAIN cloud."

He waves a wing. Monkey's cloud starts to dissolve away into rain. Monkey is soaking wet before he even hits the ground.

THE END

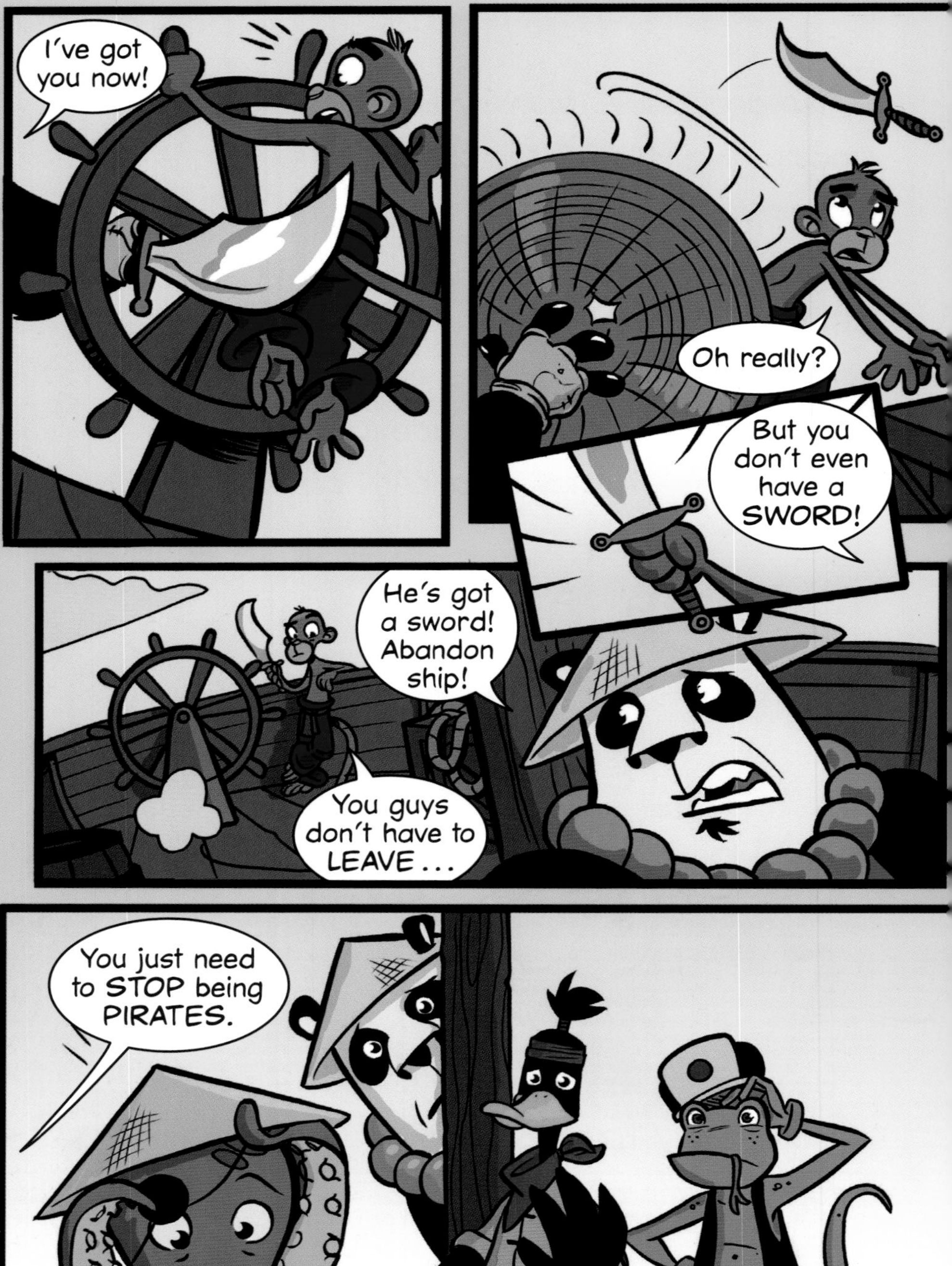
I've got you now!
Oh really?
But you don't even have a SWORD!
He's got a sword! Abandon ship!
You guys don't have to LEAVE . . .
You just need to STOP being PIRATES.

"But pirating is all we know how to do," says Octopus.

"Do you ever explore?" asks Monkey.

"Oh sure," says Lizard. "As a part of our pirate activities."

Monkey puffs out his chest. "Well," he says, "I'm actually a prince. And I think my kingdom could use an exploration ship! Who wants the job?"

All the crew raise their hands, even Captain Panda. "Good!" says Monkey. "Then let's sail together for places unknown. A grand adventure indeed!"

THE END

Monkey waves at the sky and another cloud swoops down. He jumps on it as it passes by. Xing reaches for him and swipes at him, but Monkey zips back and forth. No matter how hard Xing tries, he can't hit Monkey.

Monkey brings his cloud around in a big loop and smacks Xing as he zips by. He does it again. And again. Soon Xing, the mighty giant, is crying!

Go on to the next page.

"Please stop smacking me!" he roars. "I'll share my treasure with you!"

If Monkey stops smacking Xing,

TURN TO PAGE 18.

If Monkey tries to finish Xing once and for all,

TURN TO PAGE 39.

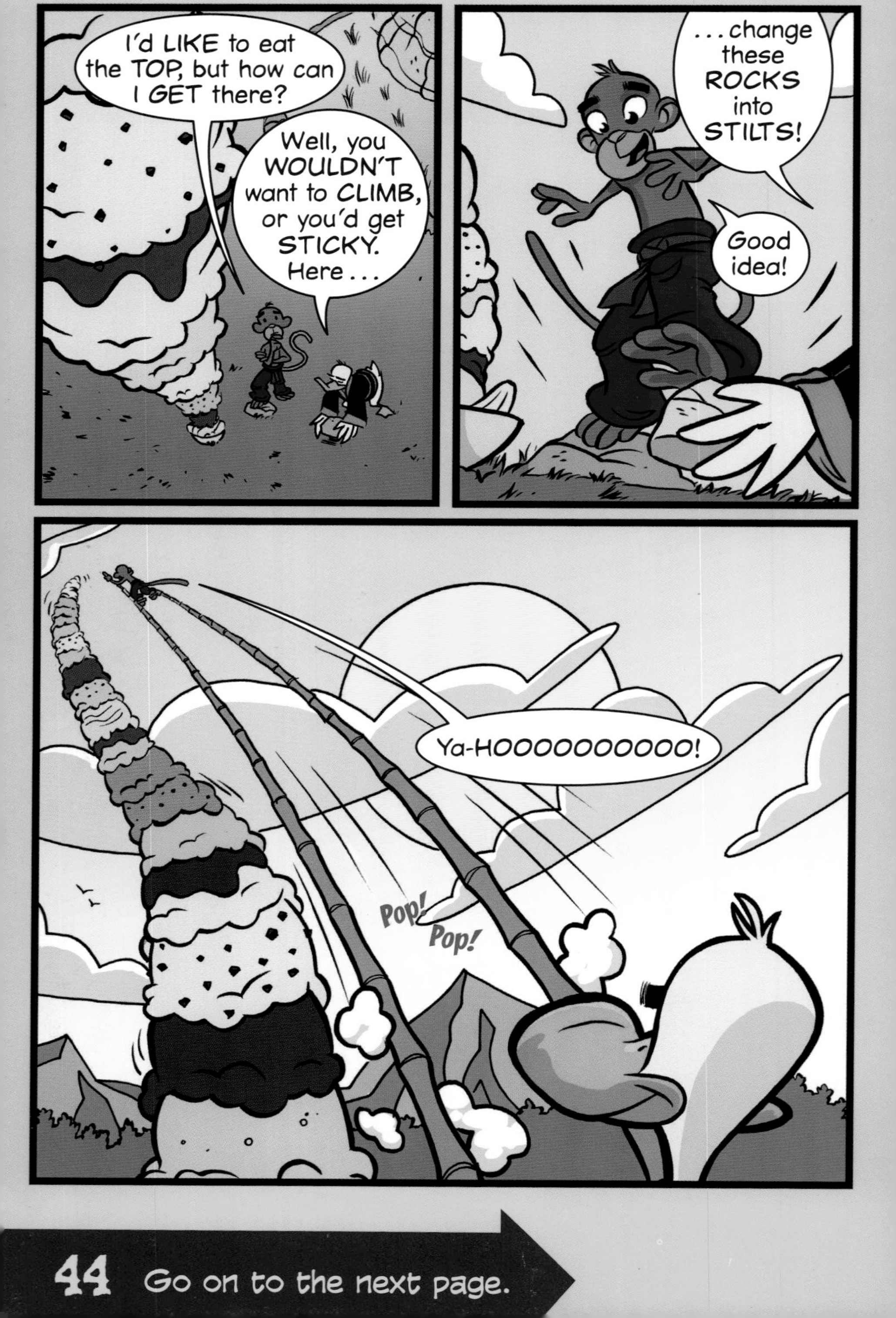
I'd LIKE to eat the TOP, but how can I GET there?
Well, you WOULDN'T want to CLIMB, or you'd get STICKY. Here . . .
. . . change these ROCKS into STILTS!
Good idea!
Ya-HOOOOOOOOOO!
Pop!
Pop!

Monkey shoots through clouds to the top. "Uh-oh," he says. "I didn't bring a spoon!"

He looks down at his stilts. "I have good balance," he says. "I really only need one stilt." He takes the other in his hand. With a "pop!" it turns into a spoon.

Monkey's balance isn't as good as he thought. He falls back and tumbles through the air!

As Monkey falls to the ground far below, he wishes he could change it into a big, soft pillow...

THE END

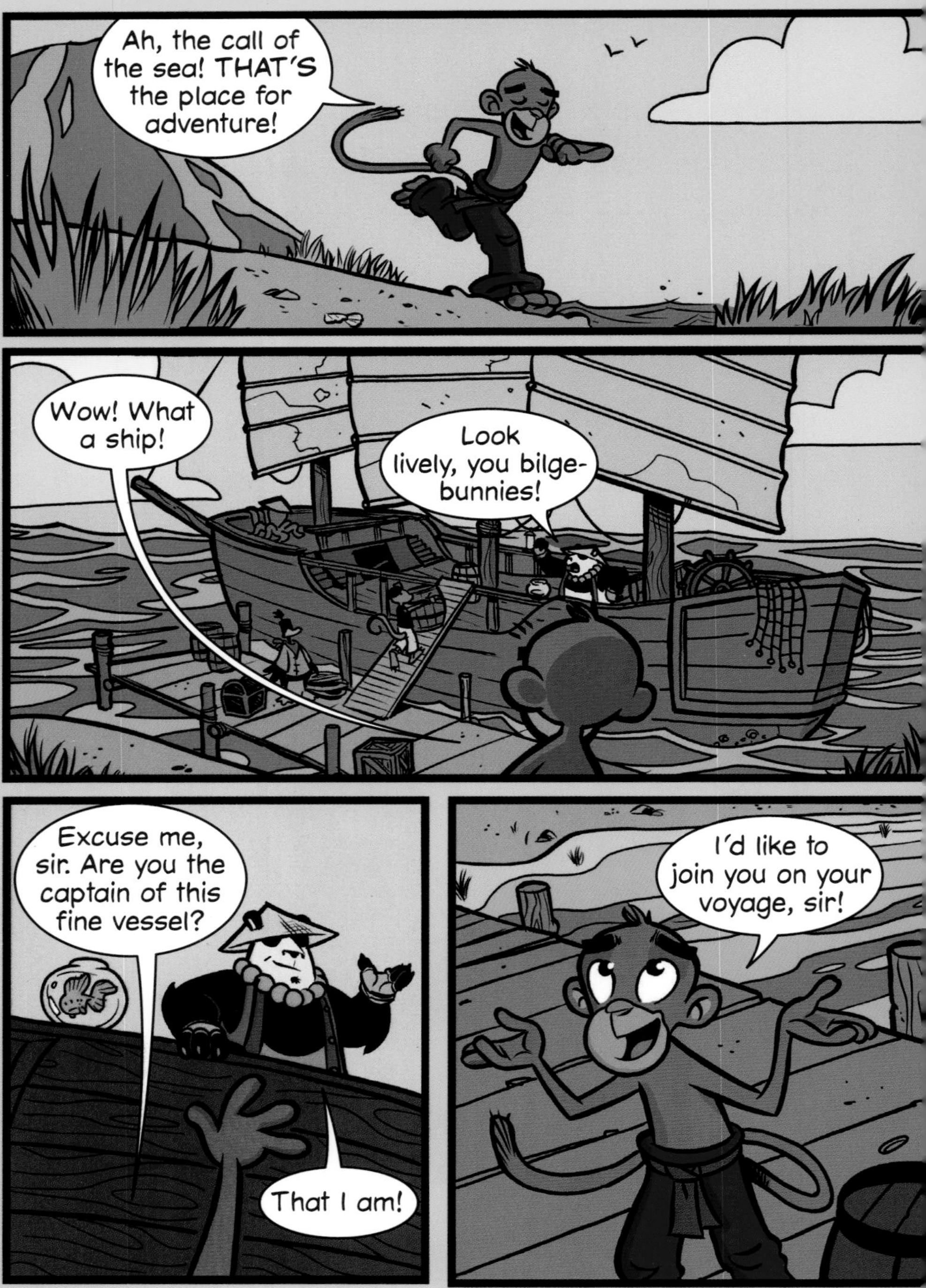
Ah, the call of the sea! THAT'S the place for adventure!
Wow! What a ship!
Look lively, you bilge-bunnies!
Excuse me, sir. Are you the captain of this fine vessel?
That I am!
I'd like to join you on your voyage, sir!

"Would you now?" The panda laughs. "Well, we're casting off. Hop aboard!"

Monkey jumps on as the ship drifts away from the dock. Soon the sails are full and the ship is tearing through the water.

"I see a sail ahead!" calls an octopus.

"Head straight for her, Mr. Octopus," growls the captain. "Mr. Lizard, Mr. *Goose*! Ready the cannons!"

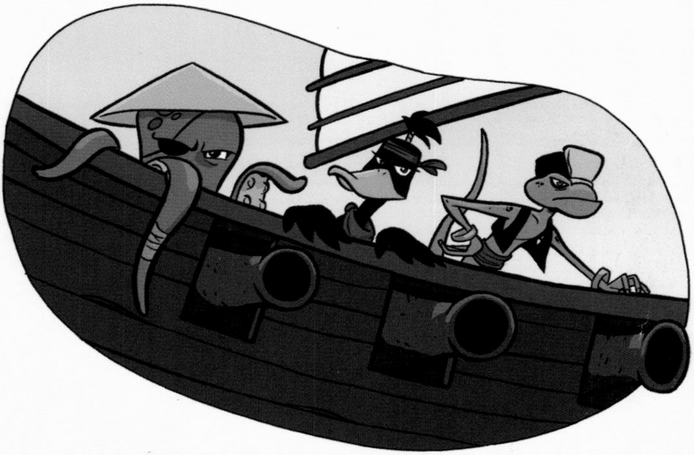

Monkey gasps. This isn't just any ship . . . this is a pirate ship!

"Little monkey, you'd better help us capture that ship!" yells Captain Panda.

Go on to the next page.

Monkey isn't sure what to do! He wanted adventure, but pirates are bad...aren't they?

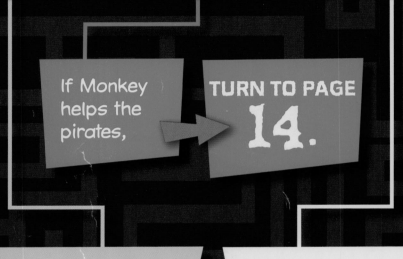

If Monkey helps the pirates,

TURN TO PAGE 14.

If Monkey fights the pirates,

TURN TO PAGE 20.

If Monkey jumps overboard,

TURN TO PAGE 37.

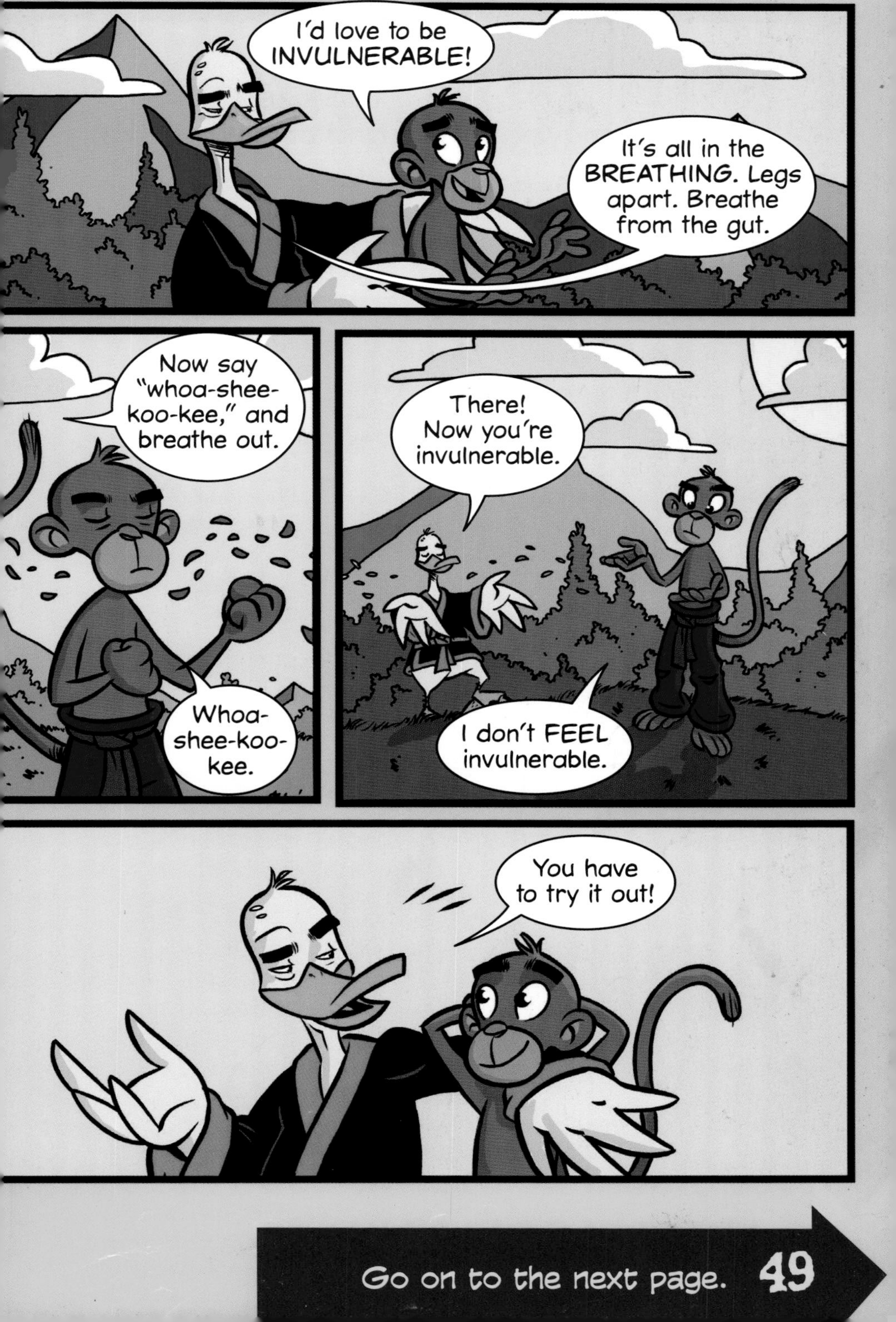
I'd love to be INVULNERABLE!
It's all in the BREATHING. Legs apart. Breathe from the gut.
Now say "whoa-shee-koo-kee," and breathe out.
Whoa-shee-koo-kee.
There! Now you're invulnerable.
I don't FEEL invulnerable.
You have to try it out!

Go on to the next page.

"You'll see!" says Duck. "Jump off the mountain, maybe. Or go and challenge Nian, the ocean lion. If Nian can't hurt you, then you'll know that you're invulnerable."

If Monkey jumps off the mountain,

TURN TO PAGE
29.

If Monkey challenges Nian,

TURN TO PAGE
7.

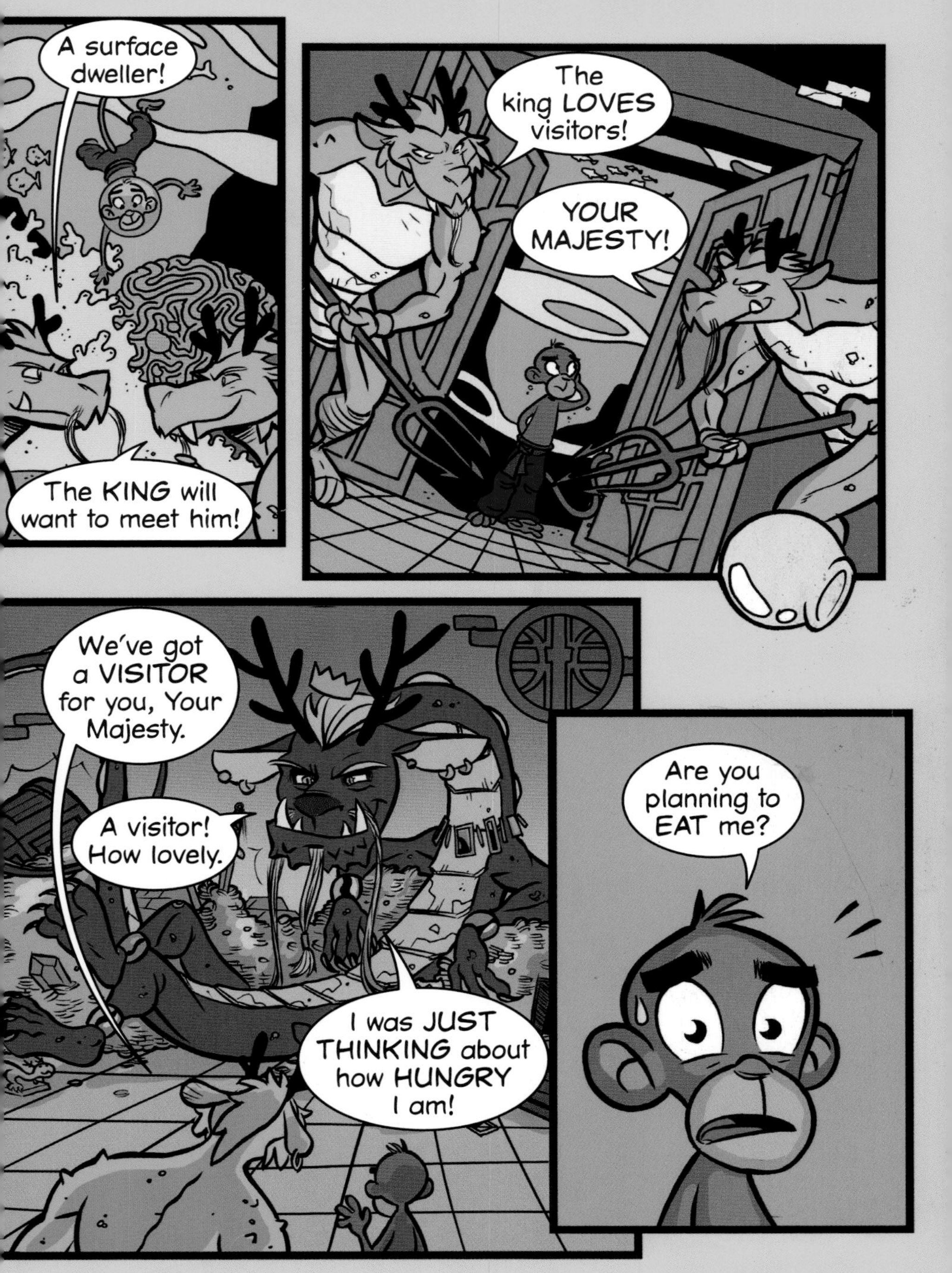

A surface dweller!
The KING will want to meet him!
The king LOVES visitors!
YOUR MAJESTY!
We've got a VISITOR for you, Your Majesty.
A visitor! How lovely.
I was JUST THINKING about how HUNGRY I am!
Are you planning to EAT me?

Go on to the next page.

The Dragon King laughs. "Eat you?" he says. "Oh goodness, no! But I never eat alone. I was hoping that you could join me!" He holds out his big, scaly hand. "Shall we?"

"Sounds good to me, Your Majesty!" says Monkey, hopping onto the king's tail. "I could use a good meal!"

THE END

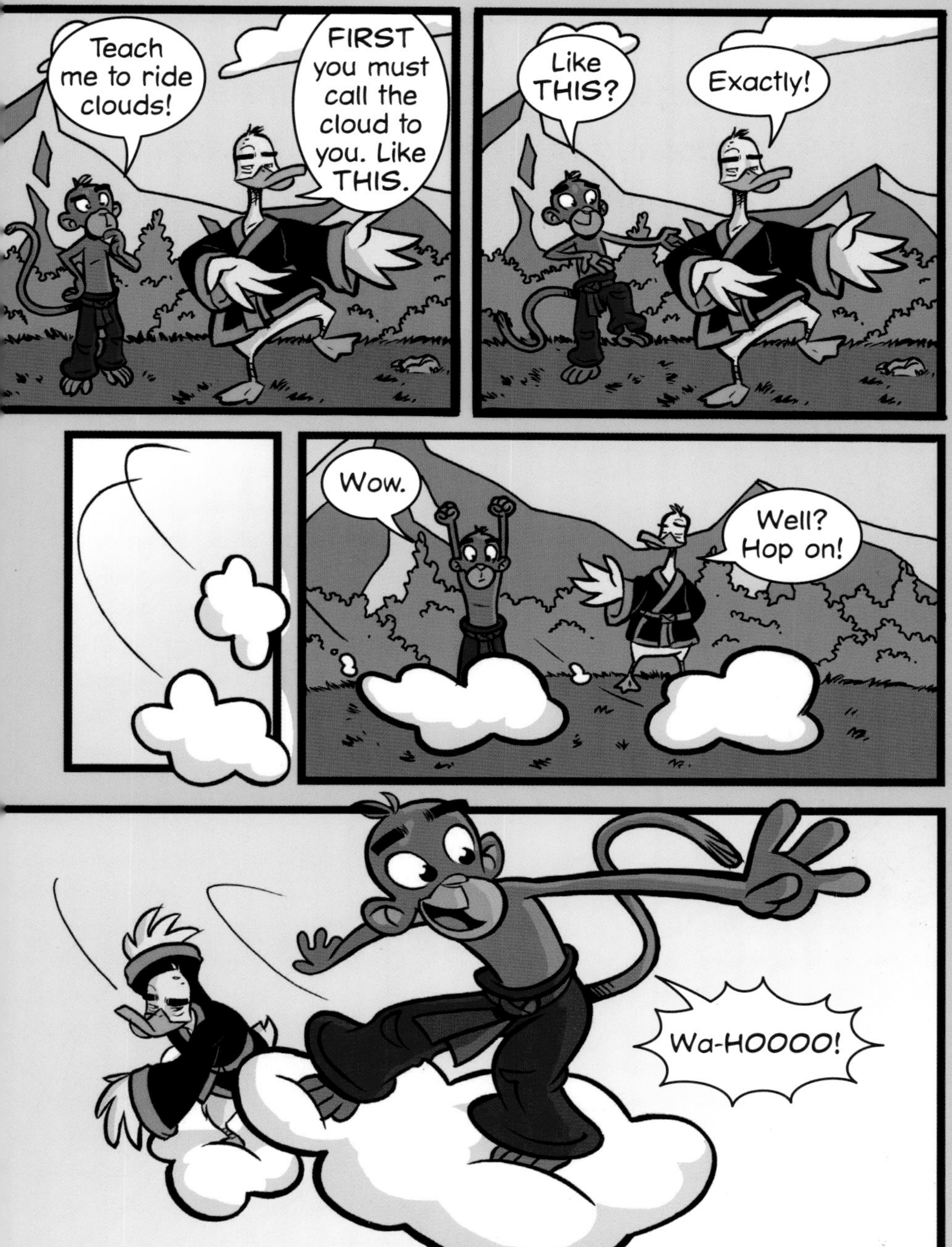
Teach me to ride clouds!
FIRST you must call the cloud to you. Like THIS.
Like THIS?
Exactly!
Wow.
Well? Hop on!
Wa-HOOOO!

Go on to the next page.

Monkey zips through the air. He feels like he was born to fly. "You're going too fast," says Duck. "First, you must practice some basic moves."

If Monkey slows down and practices,

TURN TO PAGE
9.

If Monkey decides to go faster,

TURN TO PAGE
36.

Monkey runs up to the giant creature and leaps into its mouth.

Monkey slides down Nian's gullet. "Whew!" says Monkey. "It's hot in here. And it stinks!"

He starts punching the walls of Nian's stomach. "I'm not strong enough to hurt Nian on his outside, but I can hurt him here!" he says.

Nian grabs his stomach and rolls around. With a loud "BLECH," he throws up Monkey and scurries back into the water.

Monkey saved the village... but he needs a bath!

THE END

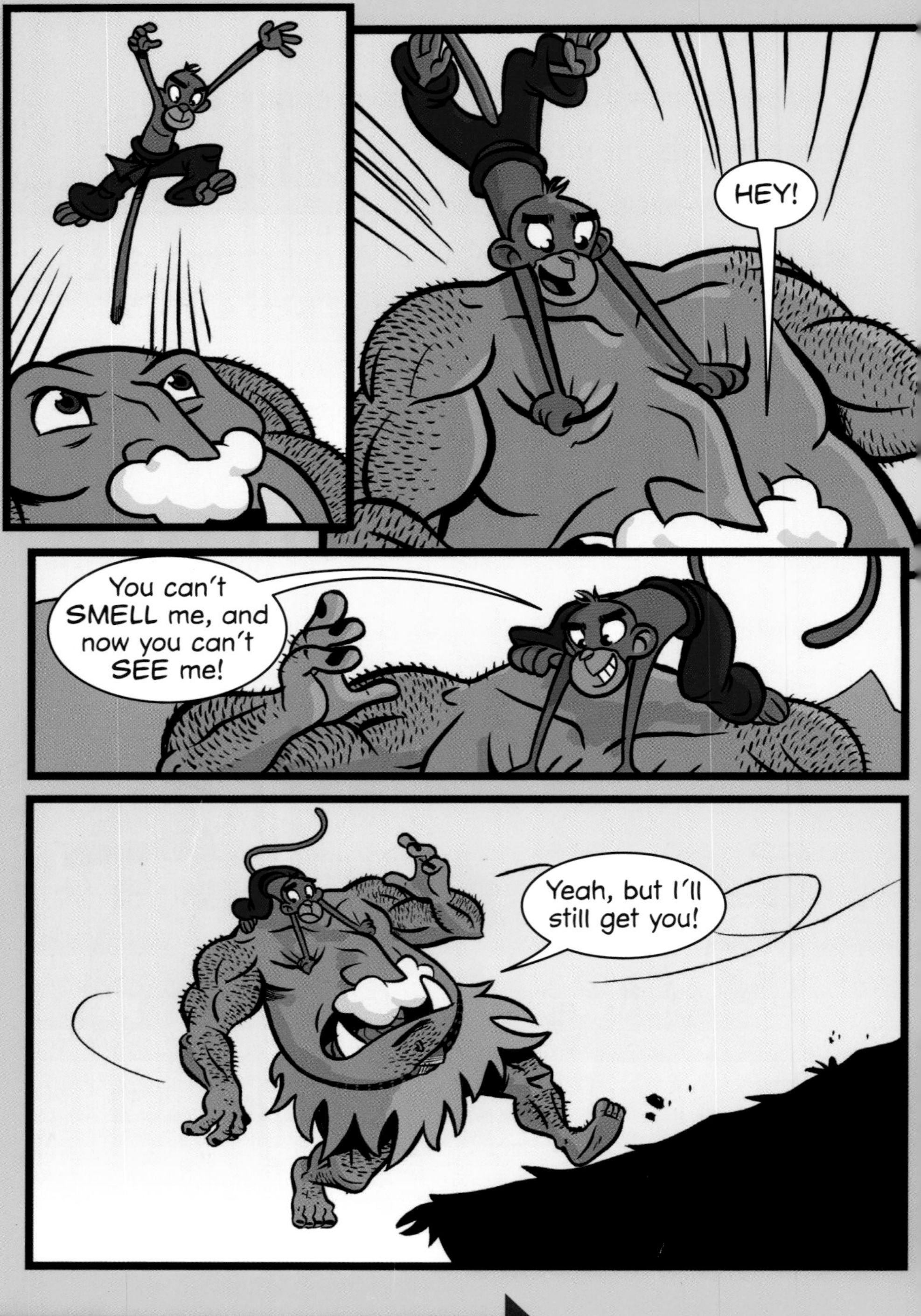
HEY!
You can't SMELL me, and now you can't SEE me!
Yeah, but I'll still get you!

Xing tries to put his foot down, but there is no ground beneath it! He tumbles backward and drops off the cliff.

Monkey plants his feet firmly on the cloud as it slips out of the giant's nose. He's about to fly away when he feels big fingers wrap themselves around his body.

As Xing falls, so does Monkey. His cloud-riding skills can't save him from the giant's mighty grip.

THE END

"I want to go back to land," says Monkey. "Life at sea is much harder than I thought it would be!"

"Then climb on my back, little not-fish," says Manta Ray. Monkey does, and Manta Ray shoots through the water faster than Monkey can believe.

Soon Monkey is within swimming distance of the shore. "Thanks, Manta Ray," says Monkey. "After all of this trouble, I think I'm happy to be a prince!"

THE END

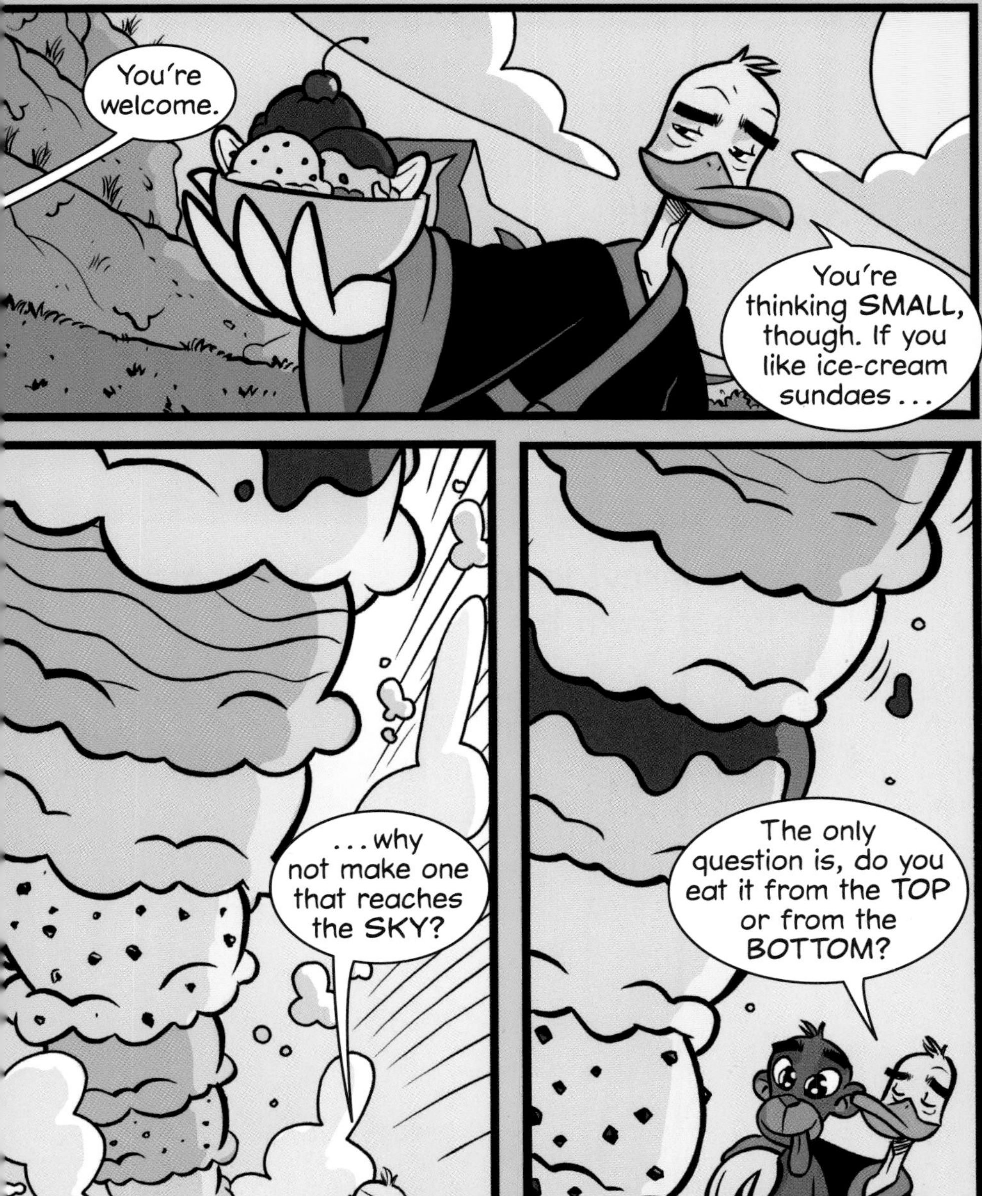
You're welcome.
You're thinking SMALL, though. If you like ice-cream sundaes . . .
. . . why not make one that reaches the SKY?
The only question is, do you eat it from the TOP or from the BOTTOM?

Monkey looks at the sundae. The top is very high up. It disappears into the clouds. It's covered in melted chocolate fudge and peanut crumbles. The bottom is made of rich ice cream and moist banana.

If Monkey decides to eat from the top,

TURN TO PAGE
44.

If Monkey decides to eat from the bottom,

TURN TO PAGE
17.

Monkey ducks behind a barrel of fish as the one-eyed general sends another thunderclap over his head. He scoops out a floppy catfish and throws it with all his might. It hits the general right in the good eye!

"I *can't see!*" yells the general. "I got catfish in my eye!"

"Don't worry," comes a voice from behind Monkey. "We'll take care of him."

Monkey has just enough time to see the other Thunder Generals swinging their clubs at him before it's

THE END

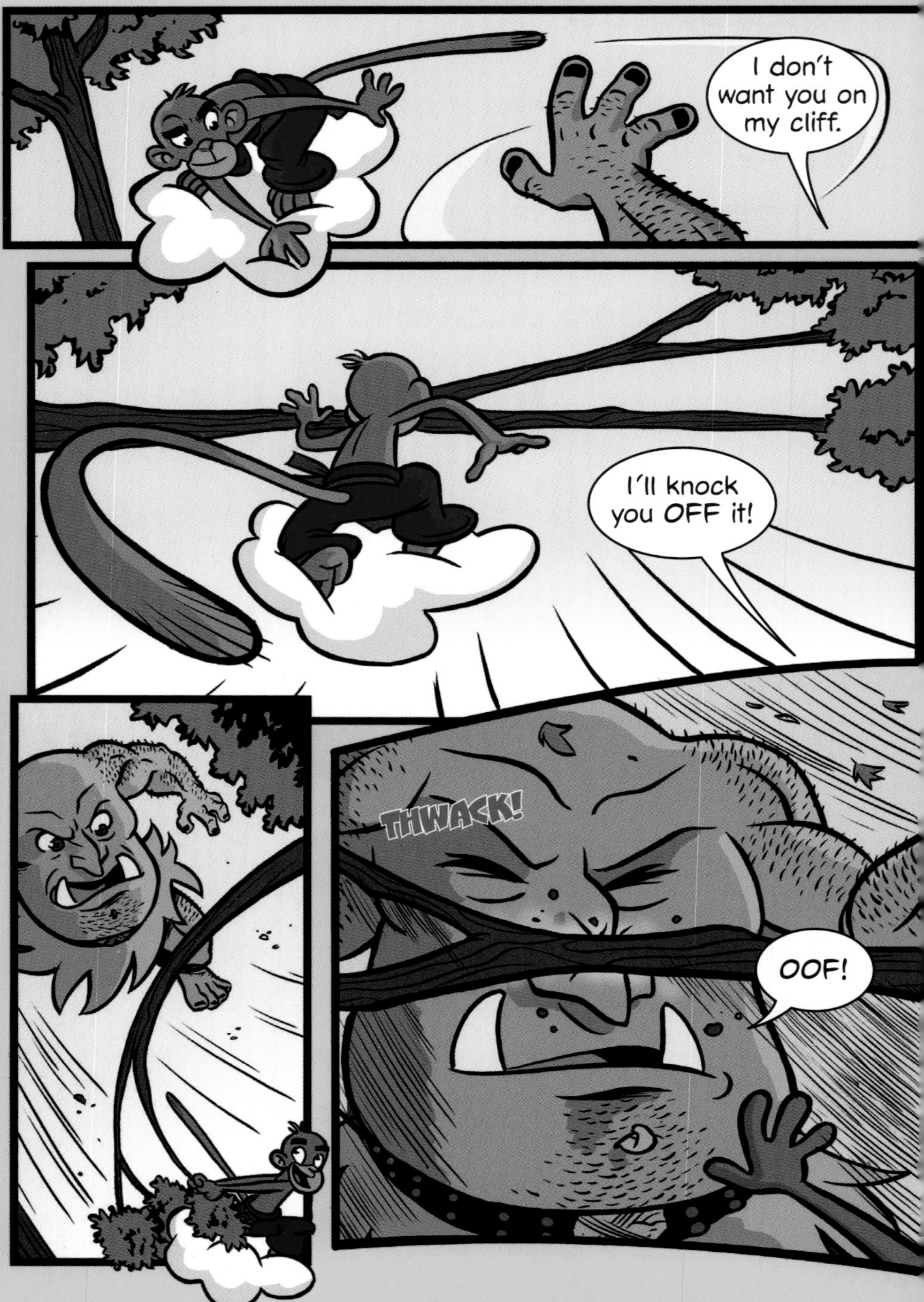
I don't want you on my cliff.
I'll knock you OFF it!
THWACK!
OOF!

Monkey flies up into the air as fast as he can. He looks back as Xing tumbles to the ground.

"Whew!" he exclaims. "I'm glad I got away from that monster. Now I'm safe to have lots of adventures. I'll ride clouds until I've seen the whole world!"

And with that, Monkey shoots off toward the horizon.

THE END

NOV   2012

The story of **MONKEY** comes from China. People told stories about Monkey for many years, but the version that we know comes from a book written in the 1590s. In the book, Monkey is a proud king. He finds out that there are people more important than himself. Monkey learns to do all sorts of amazing things so that he can become just as important. The book is an adventure story, but it is also a story about becoming more grown-up.